This year, Dad said, "It's Mom's turn
to choose."

Ben and I were very surprised and excited.
Until Mom said, "I'd like to go somewhere
nice and quiet. Some place in the middle
of nowhere."

"Oh no!" said Ben and I. "That sounds
so boring!"

"We'll stay in an old house," said Mom. "Somewhere with no traffic and no television."

"Well, maybe just a small television," said Dad. "But somewhere peaceful."

"Yes," said Mom. "A nice, quiet house in the middle of nowhere."

And that is where we ended up going.

The Middle of Nowhere

Sally Prue

Illustrated by Stephen Lewis

My family always argued about vacations.
We always wanted to go to different places.
I always wanted to go to Funworld.

"Not this year," Dad would say.

Ben always wanted to go to Water Mania.

"Not this year," Dad would say. We usually ended up going where Dad wanted to go.

It was a long way to the middle of
nowhere, and we all got hot and a little sick.
"I wish I were back at school," said Ben.
"So do I," said Dad.

We drove on and on. The road got smaller and smaller. Great big, dark trees cast shadows across the road.

At last, Mom stopped the car, and we all climbed out.

"Where are we?" asked Ben.

"The middle of nowhere," I said.

We had stopped outside an old house in the middle of the forest. The windows of the house were dark. The door looked like an angry mouth.

"It's boring," said Ben, with a gulp. "Let's go home."

There was a sign on the door. It said:
CANDLES ON THE TABLE.

Mom opened the door with a big black
key. It was quite dark inside.

"Where's the light switch?" asked Dad.

"No electricity?" asked Mom, when we'd looked all around the room.

"How can we plug in the television?" asked Dad.

"How will we see when it gets dark?" asked Ben.

"That's easy," I said. "Candles!"

There was a black pot hanging over
the fire, but there was no oven anywhere.

"Isn't it exciting!" said Dad.

Mom didn't seem so sure. Ben definitely
didn't seem sure. And Dad didn't seem sure,
either, when he found out we could only
have bread and cheese for supper.

By then it was really dark, so we lit some
candles and went to our bedrooms.

Mom and Dad's room was big and creaky.
Our room was not so big, but it was even
creakier. The flame from the candle made
black shadows jump around scarily on the walls.

I'm sure Ben was just as scared as I was,
but neither of us said so.

The bathroom was even worse. It was full
of dark holes where spiders could hide.
Or frogs, or toads.

"Or even striped snakes with big fangs,"
said Ben. "I don't think I need to go to
the bathroom."

It was cold in bed, so we wore all our clothes. The wind moaned around the house.

"What if something comes down the chimney?" asked Ben.

"It won't," said Dad.

"But what if it does?" he asked.

"It *won't*," said Dad, and he blew out our candle.

"Molly!" said Ben.

"What?" I asked.

"It's very creaky."

"But not boring," I said.

"No," said Ben. His voice wavered.

A flash of lightning lit up the room.
Thunder rumbled.

"Definitely not boring," he said.

In the morning we could see better, but everything was still old and dark and creaky.

Outside there were lots of trees. Wet, dark trees.

"What can we do?" I asked, after we'd all had some more bread and cheese.

Dad looked at Mom, and Mom looked at Dad. "Play hide-and-seek," suggested Dad.

Ben looked around at the creaky house that was full of holes and spiders. "You must be joking," he said.

Ben and I tried playing cards . . . and checkers . . . and board games.

"This is boring," I said.

"There's nothing to do," said Ben.

"Why don't you play hide-and-seek?" asked Dad, again.

"But what if the spiders get us?" asked Ben.

"Or the striped snakes?" I asked.

"You could rub Mom's face cream all over you," said Dad. "That tastes horrible. Nothing will eat you then."

Ben and I went to see Mom, but Mom said we couldn't have any face cream. She even told us to stop acting so silly!

That made us so upset that we didn't watch where we were going. We went left instead of right at the end of the hall.

"This is wrong," I said. We were in a little hall. It was even darker and gloomier than the rest of the house, and I felt a bit frightened.

There was a deer's head on the wall, and at the end of the hall was a little door.

"I don't remember that before," I said.

"What's that noise?" asked Ben suddenly.

"Your knees are knocking," I said.

The little door was very dark, and almost too small for a grown-up.

"What do you think is on the other side?" I asked.

"Snakes," said Ben. "I wish I had Mom's face cream on."

"We have to find out," I said. "If there's something horrible, it might come and get us while we're asleep."

"In the middle of the night, in the middle of nowhere!" said Ben. "And that would be the end of us!"

Slowly, we went up to the door. Slowly, we pulled the handle. Slowly, the door creaked open.

We looked–and our eyes nearly popped out! We got the surprise of our lives!

"Mom!" we shouted. "Dad!"

"Look at the lake!" said Mom.

"We can go swimming and fishing!" I said.

"Look at the cabin and the swings," said Ben.

"What a great porch and grill," said Dad.

"We can cook and eat out here!"

And you know, we had so much fun on that vacation that we all agreed to go back to the middle of nowhere again next year!